Miracle Miles and His Buddy Bunch

The Best Day Ever!

Written by Paras Bengco

Illustrated by Penny A. Booher Jones

"Hello Miles! Can you come out and play? The sky is bright blue, the sun is shining bright, and the birds are singing!" cheered Sophia.

"Can I go out and play, Mommy?" asked Miles.

"After you take your asthma treatment," his mother said.

Hi, my name is Miles, and I have asthma. Asthma is a disease that causes problems for your breathing. It affects an organ in your body called the LUNGS. Your lungs are in your chest. They take air into your body for your blood. When your lungs are normal, the air goes in and out easily. But sometimes for people with asthma, it's hard to breathe normally.

When I run around having fun, sometimes I have to stop and slow down because it's hard to breathe. Certain grasses, trees, or animals can also affect my lungs and make it hard to breathe.

When I have an asthma attack, it can be scary because air doesn't flow in and out of my lungs. Then I start coughing, wheezing, and being short of breath.

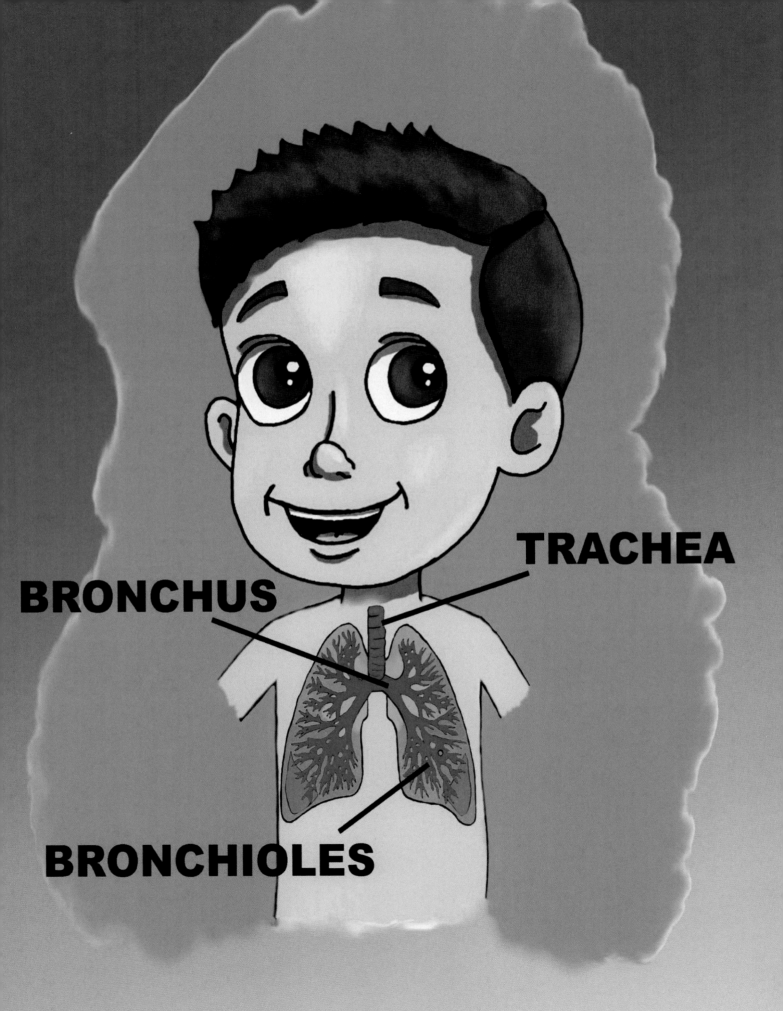

Although there is no cure for asthma, there are things I can do to help myself.

I have a nebulizer machine to help me breathe. My mom puts a medicine called Albuterol into the nebulizer.

This medicine opens up the airways in my lungs.

When I put on the mask, I breathe in the medicine and feel better. Now I'm ready to play outside.

Even though I have asthma, I can still run and play with my friends or participate in sports.

"How do you feel?" asked Sophia.

"I feel a lot better," Miles said. "But my mom said I should take it easy."

"Let's go to the park!" Sophia cheerfully shouted. "We can play on the swings!"

"Let's see who can swing the highest," said Miles. "Make sure you don't fall off and get hurt, Sophia."

As soon as Miles and Sophia swung their highest, Miles slipped off the swing and landed in the sand.

"Are you alright?" asked Sophia.

"Yeah," said Miles. "This was the best swing ever!"

As Miles and Sophia played in the sand, a cute light-colored puppy ran beside them. The puppy wagged its tail and started barking.

"Ruff! Ruff!"

"I think he's lost. We should find his owner," Miles said. "I wonder what the puppy's name is?"

"Salsa! Where are you?" yelled a little boy.

"Sophia, it's Eddie, Kim, and Leo!" shouted Miles, with enthusiasm.

Eddie, Kim, and Leo live in the same neighborhood as Miles and Sophia and they all go to the same school.

"Hi Sophia and Miles," Eddie said. "I see you met my new puppy, Salsa."

"I have an idea," said Eddie. "Why don't we build a sand castle? I can use this red cup and get water from the fountain."

Just as the sand castle was almost complete, Salsa came running and dug his paws into it. Eddie scolded his puppy. "Salsa!"

"That's okay, Eddie," smiled Miles. "That was the best sand castle ever!"

"I have an idea," said Sophia. "Why don't we ride our bikes?"

"That's a great idea!" cheered Eddie.

As the kids got on their bikes, Eddie yelled, "On the count of three, let's race to the end of the block! One, two… three!"

As the kids raced down the block, Miles' bicycle chain came off and slowed him down. He was also out of breath because he was peddling fast.

Even though Miles didn't win the race, he yelled, "That was the best bike race ever!"

Because I was peddling fast, I was having a hard time breathing. I was wheezing and couldn't catch my breath.

I quickly pulled out my asthma inhaler.

An inhaler is small and round, and gives a specific amount of medicine into my lungs. I breathe in the medicine that comes out, just like when I use my nebulizer machine.

This opens my lungs and helps me breathe easier.

"I feel so much better," said Miles.

"I have an idea! Why don't we go to my house and get a doughnut snack?"

Sophia, Eddie, Leo, and Kim quickly agreed.

Miles' mother gave them each the last of the doughnuts.

"Make sure you wash your hands before you eat your doughnuts," she said.

Before Miles could take the last bite of his doughnut, Salsa jumped up and used his paw to knock the doughnut out of Miles' hand. Salsa quickly took the last bite of Miles' doughnut.

Again, Eddie scolded his puppy. "Salsa!"

"That's okay... that was the best doughnut ever!" Miles said, his smile beaming.

"I have another idea," said Eddie. "Let's go swimming at my house."

Miles, Sophia, Leo, and Kim all smiled.

"That sounds good to us!" said Miles.

As the kids played in the pool, Eddie's father tossed in a big colored ball.

Miles, Eddie, Leo, Kim, and Sophia threw the ball back and forth to one another. As they volleyed the ball, Sophia hit it over the neighbor's fence by accident. The neighbors weren't at home so they couldn't get the ball.

Sophia felt really bad.

"It's okay, Sophia. It's not your fault," said Miles. "That was the best volleyball game ever!"

Eddie's dad asked the children if they wanted pizza. They quickly got out of the pool and changed into dry clothes. As they ate the pizza, they played with Salsa.

Salsa all of a sudden jumped on Miles and knocked down his last slice. Miles got a pizza stain on his shirt.

"Salsa!" yelled Eddie.

"That's okay," said Miles. "That was the best pizza slice ever!"

It was getting late and Miles had to go home. As Miles stepped on his skateboard, he looked back and yelled, "You all are my best friends ever!"

As Miles got ready for bed, his father asked, "How was your day?" Miles thought about everything that happened to him.

"Um, let's see... I fell off a swing. Eddie's new puppy, Salsa, destroyed our sand castle. We had a bike race and my bike chain came off so I didn't win. I had a doughnut and before I could take the last bite, Salsa knocked it out of my hands and ate it. We went swimming at Eddie's house and Sophia hit the ball over the neighbor's fence. The neighbors weren't home so we couldn't get the ball. I was eating pizza and before I could take my last bite, Salsa took it.

"But... THIS WAS THE BEST DAY EVER!"

Small moments, Big Lessons from Miracle Miles:

"When life gives you a hundred reasons to cry, show life that <u>YOU</u> have a thousand reasons to smile."

This book is dedicated to Miles Sebastian Bengco. Miles was a beautiful eleven-year-old boy who lived life to the fullest. Miles had asthma. He truly was a miracle and kept a positive attitude in everything he did. Miles was funny, witty, endearing, a social butterfly, confident, a risk taker, adventurous and had a kind spirit. He was affectionate, intelligent, loved to laugh, and loved his friends and family. Peace be to the memory of Miles' pure soul. He was my delight, my loving child, he was my world. When I awake and when I lie down, I always think of my son. His life was taken on June 19, 2013.

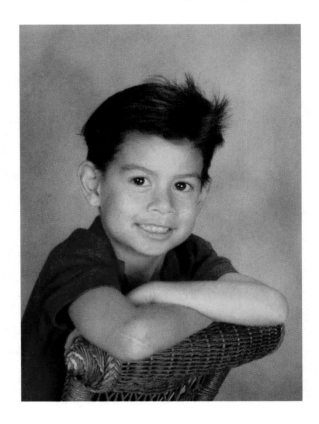

Breathe

Acknowledgments

As Miles' father, I want to thank the following:

I want to thank Rory Demeire. Thank you for your support, patience, encouragement, and love. You have been by my side since losing my son and have been the *air* to help me *'breathe'* when I thought I no longer could.

I want to thank Miles' grandparents. All four of you have helped care, nurture, teach, and have selflessly dedicated your love & time to your grandson. Miles loved all four of you so much! Mom, I know you and Miles are together. I have peace of mind knowing that my son is not alone.

I want to thank Penny Booher Jones. Penny has been part of my journey in bringing the Miracle Miles characters to life. Thank you Penny for your creativity and beautiful illustrations.

I want to thank Sherry Chamblee who helped me with the book editing and formatting. Thank you for being part of this journey.

I want to thank Harold Weitzberg with Weitzberg Consulting. It wasn't too long ago you and I sat down for a cup of coffee. From that time, you have been instrumental in helping me share my son's story. Thank you for your guidance and friendship.

I want to thank Raquel Rodriguez with R2 Media. Your marketing company is helping keep my son's memory alive and it is greatly appreciated. I also want to thank you for your guidance and friendship.

I want to thank my brothers Jon and Rick, and their wives Mischelea and Susie, for keeping our families close. I can't forget my little nephews and niece and the rest of Miles' cousins, aunts, and uncles. Miles loved you all.

Lastly, I want to thank several friends who continue to contact me with encouragement during an ordinary or special day. Me being in your thoughts and prayers is a blessing. Thank you all.

www.miraclemilesbooks.com

Made in the USA
Coppell, TX
04 March 2020